Dear mouse friends,
Welcome to the world of

Geronimo Stilton

THE RODENT'S GAZETTE
EDITORIAL STAFF

Geronimo Stilton
A learned and brainy
mouse; editor of
The Rodent's Gazette

Thea Stilton
Geronimo's sister and
special correspondent at
The Rodent's Gazette

Trap Stilton
An awful joker;
Geronimo's cousin and
owner of the store
Cheap Junk for Less

Benjamin Stilton
A sweet and loving
nine-year-old mouse;
Geronimo's favorite
nephew

HAVE A HEART, GERONIMO

WITHDRAWN

Scholastic Inc.

Copyright © 2019 Mondadori Libri S.p.A. for PIEMME, Italia, Via Mondadori 1, 20090 Segrate, Italy. International Rights © Atlantyca S.p.A. English translation © 2022 by Atlantyca S.p.A.

The publisher does not have any control over and does not assume any responsibility for author or third-party websites or their content.

GERONIMO STILTON names, characters, and related indicia are copyright, trademark, and exclusive license of Atlantyca S.p.A. All rights reserved. The moral right of the author has been asserted. Based on an original idea by Elisabetta Dami. geronimostilton.com

Published by Scholastic Inc., Publishers since 1920, 557 Broadway, New York, NY 10012. SCHOLASTIC and associated logos are trademarks and/or registered trademarks of Scholastic Inc.

Stilton is the name of a famous English cheese. It is a registered trademark of the Stilton Cheese Makers' Association.

This book is a work of fiction. Names, characters, places, and incidents are either the product of the author's imagination or are used fictitiously, and any resemblance to actual persons, living or dead, business establishments, events, or locales is entirely coincidental.

ISBN 978-1-338-80224-5

Text by Geronimo Stilton
Original title *Un amore da brivido*
Cover by Iacopo Bruno, Andrea Da Rold, and Alessandro Muscillo
Graphic Designer: Laura Dal Maso / theWorldofDOT
Illustrations by Danilo Loizedda, Carolina Livio, Daria Cerchi, and Valeria Cairoli
Translated by Anna Pizzelli
Special thanks to Anna Bloom
Interior design by Becky James

10 9 8 7 6 5 4 3 2 1   22 23 24 25 26

Printed in the U.S.A.   40
First printing 2022

A REAL HEART-STOPPER!

A **cold** breeze blew through my whiskers. Brrr! February is not my favorite time of year. I rubbed my paws together and then **hugged** my arms close to my sides.

But I'm getting ahead of myself. My name is Stilton, *Geronimo Stilton*, and I am the

It's colder than a cheddar milkshake out here!

editor in chief of *The Rodent's Gazette*, the most *famouse* newspaper on Mouse Island!

I was WALKING to the office, mentally going through my to-do list: hold a *Gazette* staff meeting, edit a few articles, review the paper's marketing plans . . . I was so caught up in my thoughts that I walked smack into a streetlight!

BAM!

Holey Swiss cheese! That was painful! Carefully, I patted my snout to make sure all my WHISKERS were accounted for.

Phew, I hadn't lost any. But my head was spinning! I stood very still, waiting for the world to stop turning.

When it did, I could see that all the rodents on the street were staring at me. How embarrassing! My fur blushed as red as a Gouda rind.

What is he doing?

Isn't that Stilton?

I darted across the street, opened the door to **The Cheddar Puff Café**, and took a deep breath. Mmmm. It smelled heavenly!

The owner spotted me and waved a paw. "Good morning, your usual today, Mr. Stilton?" he asked.

I nodded, examining all the *fabumouse* treats spread out in the display cases.

He passed me my iced mocha cheddar latte. I can't resist an **iced** drink, even in **cold** weather!

As I was unwrapping my straw, I noticed the barista had drawn a cute **heart** shape in the latte foam. As I dropped the straw in the drink, I realized that it also had a little **heart** decoration on it.

Even the sample cookies on the counter were each in the shape of a **heart**!

I took one, dunked it in my latte, and ate it up in one **BITE**. Delicious! I definitely felt better about my **embarrassing** run-in with the streetlight now.

I paid for my latte and headed for the office. Now that I had **CHEDDAR LATTE POWER**, I felt sure I could race through my to-do list before lunch!

As I was walking by the **florist's** window, I let out a squeak. They had trimmed small bonsai trees into **heart** shapes. "Oh no, here, too?"

I started walking again, but as soon as I reached the **bakery**, I stopped again. "Wow,

The florist . . .

Here, too?!

. . . the bakery . . .

Bread hearts?

. . . and the housewares store.

What's going on?

all the loaves of bread are shaped like **hearts**!"

I went a few steps farther. There were more **hearts** at the housewares store — and overnight their window had transformed into an entirely **PINK** theme. "Does everymouse have **love** on the snout all of a sudden?" I wondered out loud.

Just then, a very **cold** gust of wind caught me by surprise.

WHOOSH!

I scurried ahead a little faster. I couldn't wait to

warm up at the office. But before I got very far —

CRASH!

I walked right into a rodent carrying a very large net. The net fell open, releasing a **CLOUD** of balloons into the air, each shaped like a **heart**!

"**Frosted fontina**, more **hearts**?!? What is going on?"

But the rodent didn't seem to have heard my question. "You just made me lose my whole **balloon** delivery! You'll have to pay for these, or I'll never hear the end of it from the big cheese!"

I shrugged and pulled out my wallet to pay him.

He **stomped** away, and I stared up at the brilliant blue morning sky. The little red and pink **heart** balloons got smaller and smaller. Where had all these **hearts** come from? What did it mean? I scratched my snout thoughtfully.

Out of the corner of my eye, I noticed the time on my watch. **GREASY CAT GUTS!** Now I was late!

Whoops!

Look what you did!!!

WE ARE LIVE!

I ran the rest of the way to *The Rodent's Gazette* office. As soon as I stepped through the door, I heard the **ROAR** of a familiar voice: "There you are, Grandson! Is this the time you usually show up at work? I've been waiting here for an hour already!"

Squishy string cheese, it was my grandfather, William Shortpaws, founder of *The Rodent's Gazette*. He rambled on without waiting for an answer from me.

"What was I thinking the day I asked you to be the **editor in chief**?" he moaned.

Just then, two rodents walked by me, moving a desk. "Watch your paws, we're working here!" one of them growled.

Get out of the way!

Arg!

1

Ouch! Watch your step!

2

Help!

3

I took a step back, but . . . **BAM** . . . I knocked into another rodent, who was carrying rolls of wallpaper.

"Coming through!" he called, not stopping.

I was spun around and **BOOM**! I got a snout full of wooden ladder, and saw **STARS** for the second time that morning.

Squeak! What was going on?

Before I could ask, my cousin Trap barged in behind me. He wore a fancy black suit and a dapper bow tie.

"**Howdy**, Geronimo! I just saw you get tangled up with that ladder. You should be more careful, you know!"

I was about to reply when Benjamin and Trappy, my nephew and niece, scurried into the room. They were dressed up, too, and carried heart-shaped balloons. More **hearts**?

I turned around to ask Grandpa William for an explanation, but he was in no mood for **QUESTIONS**.

"Grandson, what are you doing still standing there? We are on a **deadline**. Follow me; you and I are having a meeting **RIGHT NOW**."

I followed Grandpa William to his office, where he lectured me on the newspaper business for almost an hour. I pretended to take notes, and eventually he ran out of

Grandson, why are you still standing there?

Hmm.

Ha, ha.

So many hearts!

steam. Finally, he dismissed me with a wave of his paw.

Relieved, I **DARTED** back out into the hallway. Two workers **rushed** up and down, looking serious. What was going on here? And why had no one told me anything about it?

I started to follow the workers, but someone tapped me on my shoulder. "Mr. Stilton, I have some documents for you to **sign!**"

I turned around to see my assistant, Mousella, holding a pen and a **huge** pile of papers. "Do I have to sign them right now?" I asked. A rodent carrying a toolbox full of nails, hammers, pliers, wrenches, and tape walked by us. I was bursting out of my fur with curiosity!

"Yes, these have to get signed today!" she said firmly.

I heaved a big sigh and proceeded to sign all the **documents**, one after the other, right there in the hallway.

When I finally finished, I handed the stack back to her. "Mousella, do you know what is going on in the office today?" I gestured around at all the construction supplies.

A look of panic flashed across Mousella's face. "Oh, um, well — oh, look, **CREEPELLA** is here!" Mousella sped off down the hall.

Creepella appeared and swept in for a
hug. "There you are! I've been looking
everywhere for you!"

"You have?" I squeaked.

"Yes, of course, come with me!" She
grabbed my **PAW** and pulled me toward
my office.

When I walked in, my **snout** dropped
open. "**Holey Swiss cheese**, can

What is going on?! Come with me!

someone please explain what is going on here?"

A whole **TV CREW** had gathered in my office!

"Now, don't get your tail in a **twist**. All you have to do is come over here and **READ** this piece of paper." Creepella led me to my desk and gestured for me to sit.

I gulped and plunked down onto my

Here they are!

desk chair. As I glanced around the room, I noticed that my sister, **THEA**, and her friend Flora were in the office, too. I was about to ask Thea what this was all about when one of the crew members flicked on a very BRɨGHT light.

Cream cheese on toast, the light blinded me! Spots swam in front of my eyes. Then I heard a voice begin to speak. "Three . . . two . . . one . . . and we are live!"

Heart to Heart!

What did that mouse say?!! We were on live TV?!? **THOUSANDS AND THOUSANDS** of rodents all over Mouse Island were watching me right now?

I started to sweat like a hunk of Parmesan left out in the sun. The paper Creepella had handed me shook in my trembling paws and I couldn't read from it.

Creepella grinned at me and signaled for me to start reading. I cleared my throat and tried to concentrate on the words in front of me. "Hmm . . . dear fellow **puppies** . . ."

The camera rodent started to **GIGGLE**. The crew members behind him exchanged confused glances. I stopped and tried again.

Dear fellow citizens

"Dear fellow citizens . . ."

Creepella smiled and FLASHED me a paws-up. She silently mouthed: "Well done."

Feeling more confident, I kept going. "Have you noticed that New Mouse City is full of **hearts**?" Suddenly, I stood up and let out a *squeak*. "I knew there was something strange going on!"

Thea sighed, Flora burst out laughing, and the camera rodent spun around in surprise and **crashed** to the ground. WHOOPS.

I could fix this. I smiled awkwardly and attempted to sit back down gracefully. When I had stood up, however, I had knocked my chair back. So when I tried to sit, I crashed to the floor like a bag of Parmesan rinds.

BAM!

My head flew back and I squashed my tail under me. This live TV experiment was now officially a **DISASTER**!

Luckily Flora revived the cameraman with stinky cheese **smelling salts**.

Creepella *RACED* over to my desk and picked up the script I had dropped. "I'll take over!" she squeaked.

She took my place as the camera mouse stood back up. "Dear fellow rodents, as Geronimo Stilton was just saying, New Mouse City has been flooded with **hearts** today. But those **hearts** are not just here to remind you that *Valentine's Day* is around the corner."

I was **impressed**. Creepella sounded like a real TV professional.

She continued, "Those **hearts** are here to mark a very important announcement. You're hearing it here first, mice: In just a few days' time, I will be opening my very own dating and wedding planning agency! Right here in *The Rodent's Gazette* offices."

My snout dropped open. WHAT?!?

HEART TO HEART

Creepella threw open her arms and a banner bearing the agency's name unfurled from the ceiling. Confetti rained down on us. Slowly I stood, trying to make sense of Creepella's announcement. I rubbed my **SNOUT** and winced.

Creepella continued to smile into the

I will be opening my very own dating and wedding planning agency!

Really?!?

camera. "Are you looking for the **cheese** to your *cracker*? Have you already met your perfect pairing? Do you want to plan a **dream** wedding? Would you like the biggest wedding CHEESECAKE ever made? Heart to Heart can do all that for you — and MORE!"

The BRIGHT lights flashed off. My whiskers *tingled*. I didn't want to be a worryrat, but I had a bad feeling about this new scheme of Creepella's.

Squeak!

Heart to Heart

Meet your rodent soul mate!

Our staff will plan a series of romantic dates with eligible mouselets. Join our rewards program and get a free cheese plate!

Plan the perfect wedding with us! Try our "Full Heart" service:

- 🖤 Selection of clothing, rings, and shoes for the big day.
- 🖤 Reservation of a fabumouse location.
- 🖤 Catering provided by the best of Mouse Island.
- 🖤 Cakes prepared by world-renowned bakers.
- 🖤 A honeymoon anywhere on Mouse Island!

Party Time!

All the crew mice started to pack up their equipment. Creepella clasped her 🐾🐾🐾🐾 together and turned to me. "Now it's time to start preparing for today's grand opening party!"

"What is going on?" I asked.

Just then, Grandpa William poked his **SNOUT** into my office. "There you are! Clean up this mess and *let's shake our tails*! It's time to put the latest issue to bed!" He disappeared back into the hall, and I shrugged at Creepella.

Fortunately, Trap came to the rescue. "Don't worry, Creepella, I will help you **organize** the *party*!"

"Fabumouse! Thanks, Trap," Creepella cried, and rushed out the door with Trap in tow. "Don't be a worryrat. I will explain more later!"

The film crew left as well. I looked around in a **daze**. With a sigh, I sat back down at my desk. **THE NEWS WAITS FOR NO MOUSE!** I needed to finish up this issue of the paper — or I'd never hear the end of it from Grandfather!

That night was the grand opening party for Creepella's new business. I wasn't thrilled about going, but it was downstairs at *The Rodent's Gazette* offices, so I had no excuse to skip it.

When I arrived, the **CELEBRATION** was in full swing. The rodents of New Mouse City had showed up in their *fanciest* outfits. Sheepishly, I looked down at my **wrinkled**

suit. I wondered if I had time to go home and change.

"Geronimo!" Trap shouted. "You **cheddarhead**, what are you wearing? Never mind! Go get something to eat — all the food is mouserific!" He darted off back into the **crowd** of guests, and I made my way to the buffet.

Before I could get to the buffet, Creepella **SPOTTED** me.

Hmmm, I . . . come with me!

"Geronimo, you're finally here! I can't wait to tell you everything!"

I was starving! "Yes . . . but . . . maybe first I should have . . . a **CHEESE TART**!"

Creepella didn't seem to hear me. She **DRAGGED** me away from the buffet. "I am just so proud of this opening party! It was a lot of work to make *The Rodent's Gazette* offices look presentable enough, you know."

I grimaced, but Creepella kept talking.

"I had planned for my agency's main office to be headquartered in **Skull Castle**, but it was infested by rock termites."

Just then, my stomach growled from hunger.

GRRRROWLLLL!

"What's that weird noise?" Creepella asked.

YIKES. I had to eat something fast!

I tried to sneak off toward the buffet

again, but Creepella held tightly to my arm and continued her story. "While waiting for the exterminators, I asked Grandpa Willie if my agency's headquarters could be here at *The Rodent's Gazette*, at least temporarily! He was so kind and said yes immediately!"

Thea and Flora came over, sipping **cheese shakes**. They looked delicious!

GRRRROWLLLL!

There went my stomach again, oh dear.

Flora leaned in and gave Creepella a **hug**. "Oh, Creepella, this agency is such a great idea!"

"I am positive it will be mouserifically successful!" Thea agreed. "No one in New Mouse City is doing anything like this!"

Suddenly, the **heart-shaped clock** hanging

above the door started to strike the hour.

Ding ding ding ding · · ·

It rang out **ten** times and then went silent.

Creepella picked up a GLASS and tapped it with a spoon. "Mouselets, may I have your attention, please?" All EYES turned to her.

"Welcome, dear rodents! I am so **happy** you are here tonight! I would like to thank every mouse who has helped me embark on

May I have your attention, please?

this new **ADVENTURE**!" The room erupted into applause.

"I'm so excited this is finally coming together for her!" Flora whispered to Thea.

Thea smiled. "Me, too. This has been her dream for so long."

They both **GIGGLED**.

It was nice to see them so happy for their good friend!

"Special thanks go to Geronimo Stilton," Creepella continued.

Why would I be getting special thanks? I plastered a half smile on my snout and turned to see what Creepella was going to say.

"Geronimo has been my ROCK of Parmesan, my wall of Gouda, my cheese knife of all trades. That's why I'm so pleased to announce that he will be joining my team as a Romance Consultant."

Squeak! I was so surprised, I nearly swallowed one of my own whiskers. What did I know about romance? But the room cheered, and Creepella hugged me. I guess I would find out exactly how much I know about romance . . . tomorrow.

DON'T SLEEP ON ROMANCE!

The party lasted until late into the night. It felt like I had been asleep for only a few minutes when a **LOUD** noise woke me up.

RING!!!

I opened one **EYE**. Then the other **EYE**. It was my alarm clock! "I am so sleepy!" I turned it off and rolled over.

RING!!!

Squeak! There was another **alarm clock** on my bedside table, with the Heart to Heart logo on it.

Chocolate-dipped string cheese, of course!

I suddenly remembered: Creepella had **GIVEN** it to me the night before, at the party, as a token of appreciation for accepting a job with her.

I'm so sleepy!

When I'd tried to tell her I didn't know anything about love or romance, she had just laughed. "You're going to be fine," she'd said, and **BOOPED** me on the snout.

I heaved myself out of bed and started to get ready. I hoped she was right!

As soon as I walked into *The Rodent's Gazette* (and Heart to Heart) offices, I saw Creepella and Grandpa William both waiting **impatiently** for me.

"There you are, finally! Hurry, we have so much to do!"

"Grandson, you have to work on the newspaper issue as well! Come on, shake your whiskers."

Squeak! My whiskers were shaking all right. With stress! How was I going to get everything done?

Creepella steered me to my office chair and piled a stack of paper onto my desk. "Here are all the applications for our services. We're so in demand, we get to choose the lucky rodents who will work with us."

I groaned.

"Don't pout. The advertising worked! This is

just what we wanted!"

I started flipping through the applications. There was a request for a fairy-tale **wedding** with a cake shaped like a castle. Then there was one for a snowy **wedding** on the top of Mount Mouserest, followed by a honeymoon on Limburger Island.

There were also **PLENTY** of mice who were looking for their soul mates and wanting Creepella's matchmaking services.

While I **READ**, Creepella made phone call after phone call. She talked to cake designers, stylists, wedding planners — any rodent who was a big name in **romance** got a call from Creepella. She was determined to work with the cream cheese of the crop!

Suddenly, Mousella poked her snout through the doorway. "Mr. Stilton, your staff rodents are in a **meeting**. We are all waiting for you!"

I glanced down at my watch. Burned cheese niblets, I was so late!

"Tell them I'm on my way!" I cried, starting to gather my things.

When I walked into the conference room, my colleagues bombarded me with questions and requests:

"Mr. Stilton, can I cut the word count on this **article**?" Stella Ratoni asked.

"Mr. Stilton, my **exposé** on feta factories is so exciting, your whiskers will fall out!" Beebe Bonbon exclaimed.

Jimmy Dribbles chimed in next. "You have to check out my post-match analysis of the latest **CHAMPIONSHIP GAME** . . . it's

fabumouse!"

I sighed. "Let's go through everything again, **slowly** this time!"

Just as we were finishing up, CREEPELLA rushed through the door. "Geronimo, you have to come back right now!"

The whole day I felt like a hamster on a wheel. I had to rush between newspaper tasks and helping Creepella, with no breaks in between.

When I finally finished up, it was already late at **NIGHT** and the office was deserted.

WHAT A DAY!

Tomorrow, it would start all over, **bright** and early. I headed home to drink a nice cup of hot cheddar tea and get a good night's sleep.

Don't Be a Worryrat, Geronimo!

A week later, when I arrived at the office, Creepella met me in the lobby again. "I have your **uniform** all ready to go!" she cried.

My uniform?

My whiskers wavered. Uniform? Then I smacked my snout with a paw. I had totally forgotten — today was the very first **wedding** event hosted by Heart to Heart.

I changed into the uniform and followed Creepella back

outside to her car.

When we arrived at the wedding location, the bride and groom ran right over to us. "Creepella, there are no mouselets here yet and it's already ten o'clock!"

They wrung their paws in concern.

I looked around. The very fancy castle was strangely empty.

Creepella turned to me and whispered, "You did remember to include the time on the invitations, right?"

GULP. I started to sweat. "Hm . . . let me check." I pulled out my

What a cheesebrain!

Well . . . actually . . .

tablet and searched for the email invitation I had sent out to their guest list. "Oh no . . ." I muttered as quietly as I could. "It looks like I actually put ten p.m. instead of ten a.m.!"

The bride's eyes grew **WIDE**. I braced for her reaction.

"Cream cheese for brains! You've ruined everything! I got up at three a.m. this morning to get ready! The early castle light is perfect!" Her eyes welled up with tears, and my fur blushed as red as a Gouda rind. This was **awkward**.

Creepella **smoothly** took over. "I'm so sorry about my associate's unfortunate error. But I have a fabumouse idea!" She gently nudged me out of the bride's eye line and pulled a tissue from her pocket.

The bride carefully dabbed her eyes and sniffled. "Yes?"

"Geronimo here will call all your guests and get them here for eleven." Creepella shot **DAGGER** eyes in my direction. "And in the meantime, we will have a special extended photo shoot — the extra time and additional backgrounds **FREE** of charge, of course."

"Wonderful!" the bride said, finally smiling now.

Creepella hustled the bride and groom away with the photographer and I called all the guests **one** by **one**.

Fortunately, all the rodents were **happy** to come early. Soon the **castle** was filled with excited rodents.

Creepella came up next to me, having finished her photo session. "I really hope everything goes **perfectly** from now on!"

I had hoped so, too, but unfortunately that wasn't the case . . . I had planned

welcoming drinks in the garden because the surroundings were so spectacular, but it was February, and it was **freezing**.

Luckily, Creepella found some **blankets** to hand out to the guests. "An **OAEEIIF** party is the latest **fashion**; you're so lucky to be attending one!" she told every mouse.

"What is an **OAEEIIF** party?" a **curious** guest asked.

Creepella smiled. "It stands for: Open Air Event, Even If It's Freezing."

Whoops!

The guests giggled. "What a fabumouse idea!" one of them cried.

After the welcome reception, all the rodents filed in for the service. Then dinner was served. Finally, it was time for **cake**.

The bride and groom had specially requested a showstopper dessert. The cake was a massive ten stories!

I leaned in to get a closer look, but WHOOPS! I tripped over my own tail and bumped into the giant cake stand. The dessert fell over, right on the bride's dress. What a **disaster**!

Before the bride could even react, Creepella had **swooped** in. "Geronimo, call the **Cheddar Puff Café**. Order fifty mini cheesecakes. I will take care of the **dress**!"

I did as I was told, and shortly after, all the guests were munching delicious

CHEESECAKES. The bride happily hugged her groom in a cool, shortened version of her wedding gown.

Creepella winked at me. "Only the lower part of the dress was ruined . . . and I am a *fabumouse seamstress*!"

Melty mozzarella, even after all that had gone wrong, the wedding was a success . . . BUT CERTAINLY NOT THANKS TO ME!

X MARKS THE MYSTERY

On the way back to the **OFFICE**, Creepella tried to make me feel better. "Don't be such a worryrat. All any mouse will remember is how unique the event was. And next time you will do better, I'm sure!"

Next time? Squeak!

When we got back to *The Rodent's Gazette* office, Trap was waiting for us.

"I can't believe you knocked a whole cake over, Geronimo!" Trap called. "Creepella, you should have picked me as your Romance Consultant."

How did he already know about that??

Creepella **shrugged**. "I might have

texted him a picture," she admitted.

"I would be a mouserific associate, Creepella," continued Trap. "I have so many connections in the restaurant world! For delicious **fish** meals, I know Teddy Troutman. For unforgettable **desserts**, I know Guff Silverton, who builds life-sized cabins out of gingerbread —"

"Thank you, Trap," Creepella interrupted. "I'm sure you'd be **great**, but Geronimo is doing just fine. We're just working out some **bugs**. Every new business has some **BUMPS** along the way."

Creepella's words made me feel a **little**

bit better. At least she didn't think I had totally **ruined** everything.

I pushed past Trap and headed to my office. I had to check in on the **new** issue of *The Rodent's Gazette*.

Grandfather William had been taking care of everything at the office so that I could fully dedicate myself to **helping** Creepella.

When I walked into my office, Grandpa was waiting for me. "Don't worry about a thing, **Grandson**! Everything is going well. After all, I am the **founder** of this paper, so I know a thing or two about getting an issue out." He chuckled to himself. "Go ahead and take the rest of the

Everything is going well!

day to help Creepella. I'll keep everything **running** on this end."

He shooed me out of my own office with a wave of his paw. Unwillingly, I left and headed to the Heart to Heart area.

Creepella already had a new assignment for me. I needed to match two rodents looking for their **SOUL MATES** and then plan their **perfect** date.

I started going through the singles' profiles, mumbling to myself. "Hmm. She could be the perfect **SOUL MATE** for . . ." Suddenly my eyes happened to glance at a **FOLDER** on Creepella's desk. It was labeled: **CASE X**. How **mysterimouse**!

I couldn't help myself. I had to know what was inside. I'm an investigative reporter, after all. I jumped up and extended my **PAW** to grab it, but then Creepella **stormed** over.

"Paws off that file, Geronimo!" she cried. "What's in there is none of your **cheesewax**!"

"Cheese, Louise," I muttered. I had only wanted a **tiny** peek.

What could be in that file that was so **TOP SECRET**? I had to know! But how could I get another look?

I sighed. For now, it was time to put my **SNOUT** to the **GRINDSTONE** and find love for two deserving mouselets!

A Very Important Rodent

The following day was an **important** one for the **Heart to Heart** agency. A Very Important Rodent was coming in to speak to Creepella about her matchmaking service.

Creepella rushed around the offices. "Is everything ready?"

"Yes, I think so . . ."

I had come in early that morning to clean up a bit. I set out a tray of **cheese** and **crackers** and a pitcher of sparkling water. Creepella wanted all the details to be just right.

Countess Lara von Brie was a high society staple in New Mouse City. If she was happy with the job Creepella did for her, she'd be the **Best** advertising Creepella could get.

On the phone, the countess had told Creepella she was looking for a neat, smart, and friendly rodent. Easy cheesy, right?

When she walked in, her jasmine and smoked gouda perfume filled the air. The countess used to be a *famous* opera singer, and even when she spoke she sounded like she was singing.

"Gooooood moooorning!" she trilled.

"Good morning to you!" Creepella replied, showing her to a **comfortable** chair. "We are so happy to have you here today. Would you like a pecorino tea?"

"That would be **lovely**," she said.

Creepella pointed a paw at me. "Countess, I would like you to meet Geronimo Stilton."

Who is this cheddarhead?

Whoops!

I hurried over to offer her my , but tripped over the carpet and rolled across the floor like a dropped cheese dumpling.

Ooof . . .

She stood up from her chair, looking **ANGRY**. "Who is this cheddarhead? He better not be the soul mate you talked about on the phone!"

Creepella quickly jumped in. "Of course not! Countess, Geronimo is my *Romance*

! The rodent we chose for you is waiting for you in a **fabumouse** location . . . and he can't wait to meet you!"

Lara von Brie sighed. She tightened her shawl around her shoulders. "Then what are we waiting for!"

Creepella and I exchanged a glance and a shrug.

"**NOTHING!**" Creepella squeaked. "We can scurry over there right now!"

For the extra-special date, we had reserved balcony seats at the **New Mouse**

City Conservatory. There, a concert by the famouse pianist Ludwig von Rattenberg would take place.

When the countess stepped out of the limousine we had rented for the occasion, she swooned at the chosen location.

"This is just mouserific!"

I am mesmerized.

I am enchanted, too ...

Her date, noblemouse Joseph Cheeses, waited for her at the reserved balcony seats. He lived in a castle by Crust Port.

As the countess approached, Joseph knelt down and elegantly kissed her paws. "*Enchanted* to meet you!" he said.

The countess's fur turned pink. "I am *enchanted* to meet you, too."

Within a few piano notes, their love had blossomed. So much so that the countess waved us away, singing

"I think we can take it from here!"

A Mysterimouse Letter

That evening, Creepella and I held a party for all our friends to **CELEBRATE** how well the start of Creepella's business was going.

"Uncle Ger, Creepella says you've been a fabumouse help," my nephew Benjamin said. "Who knew that you'd be good at wedding planning and matchmaking!"

Grandpa William chimed in, too. "To be honest, you've done a pretty good job, Grandson. But don't forget your newspaper duties! Tomorrow you have to review the latest edition of *The Rodent's Gazette*!"

Just then, Mousella ran in. "Creepella, here is a letter for you!"

Creepella looked at the envelope. "Hmm, there is no **return address**. I wonder who sent it."

Creepella **RIPPED** open the envelope and read the letter inside.

Dear Creepella,

I regret to inform you that you have made a terrible mistake! The rodent you chose as your Romance Consultant is not up to the job.

If you haven't yet realized that he's as useless as a fork at a soup party, you will soon. It's time for him to prove himself!

I am giving him three challenges. If he does not succeed at just one of them, he doesn't deserve to be your associate anymore.

Sincerely,
A concerned admirer

As Creepella finished reading, Flora clasped her paws together. "An admirer! So **romantic**!"

Creepella shrugged. "I don't need a **nosy** secret admirer butting into my business. Geronimo is doing a great job . . . **mostly** . . ." She trailed off.

Thea nudged me in the ribs with her elbow. "This is a great opportunity to show every rodent that you can be just as fabumouse as Creepella thinks you are!" she said.

"That doesn't seem necessary," I said.

"Wait!" Creepella squeaked. "I've had a *fabumouse* idea. This could be mouserific publicity for the business. We'll tell everyone about the secret admirer's challenge. You'll win, Geronimo, of course. And then the whole city will be invested in my **romance** business and want my services!"

"I—I—I—I don't know, Creepella," I STAMMERED.

"He'll do it!" Thea jumped in. "Won't you, Geronimo?"

I smiled weakly and nodded.

Creepella hugged me, and all the mouselets in the room CHEERED.

What in the name of toasty cheese croutons was I getting myself into? Who was this admirer?

And what were the challenges going to be??

THE FIRST CHALLENGE

The following **MORNING**, Mousella opened the door to my office and poked her snout in. "Mr. Stilton, there is a letter for you!"

Was this the first challenge? With shaking paws, I opened the envelope. Mousella hovered in the doorway. "So, what is it?" she asked.

The envelope contained a map of New Mouse City marked with an **X** on a location in the western outskirts of the city. The directions were written right below the **map**.

When I finished reading, my whiskers started to **shake**.

For the first challenge, you must climb a steep climbing wall. Go to the location marked with the X this afternoon and steal someone's heart!

A climbing wall?
I'm scared of heights!

When I described the task to **Mousella**, she let out a squeak. "Great. I'll go get Creepella!"

The whole office went with me to see me attempt my CHALLENGE. When we arrived at the climbing wall, my whole body trembled, from paws to whiskers. **"HOLY CATS!"** I was staring at a **STEEP** — very **STEEP** — climbing wall.

To make things worse, Creepella had called in a camera crew. Whatever happened, it would be broadcast for rodents all over New Mouse City to see!

GULP.

"Don't be a worryrat, Geronimo," Creepella said. You're going to be great!"

Easy cheesy for her to say — she wasn't the rodent doing the climbing! As I started a series of stretches to get ready, a newsmouse headed our way.

"Tell me, Creepella, if Geronimo fails all the challenges, will you **FIRE** him, as requested by your admirer?"

"Hmm . . ." Creepella hesitated. But then

she went on, "That won't be a problem because I'm sure that Geronimo will not fail any of these challenges! So sure, in fact, that YES! If he doesn't succeed, he will no longer be my associate!"

Wait! What?! Rancid ricotta dumplings!

The reporter faced the **camera**. "You heard that, dear viewers!"

In the meantime, Thea handed me all the necessary equipment for my climb. "Put this on!" She placed her **PAWS** on my shoulders. "Remember to keep breathing. Look before you place your paws. It's not a *RACE*, so take your time. Most importantly — ***don't look down***!"

Squeak!!

"I always say you're a scaredy-mouse, but those are just jokes. Deep down, I know you are very brave."

I blinked back a tear.

Thea clapped her paws together. "Time to get your tail to the top of that tower!"

The climbing crew got me buckled into my harness. I took a **deep** breath and started my climb.

First one paw, then another. Go slow. This was **terrifying**!!

From the ground, Creepella CHEERED me on. "You can do it! Don't look down!"

I instinctively lowered my eyes. Very big mistake. Huge.

I am so scared!

Squeaakkkk!

When I looked down and saw all those rodents below me, very, very small, and those TV cameras, very, very far away, I realized just how very, very high up I was. I started trembling all over like mascarpone jelly.

Thea might think I'm brave, but I didn't feel very brave in that moment!

In the crowd below, Benjamin cheered me on. "Come on, Uncle Geronimo. Look up and you can do it!"

My nephew's voice gave me the **strength** to continue. In no time, I had reached the top of the climbing wall. There I spotted a small pink **heart**.

I reached out with my paw, grabbed it, and . . . **SWIIIISH!**

The **heart** was covered in **jelly**!

It slipped right out of my paw, off the side of the climbing wall, and down into the back of a passing **garbage** truck.

The crowd **ROARED** with disappointment as I looked down in horror.

Once back down on the ground, I complained loudly. "I've been set up! The **heart** was covered in slippery **jelly**."

But facts were facts. I had failed the first challenge!

You Can Do It!

I could no longer walk down the streets without some mouselet stopping me: reporters, store owners, **New Mouse City** citizens.

"How does it feel to look like a cheddarhead on live TV?" a bicyclist shouted at me while I was taking a walk in the park.

"Any news on the second challenge?" my librarian asked me.

MELTY MOZZARELLA, all anyone could talk about was the three challenges!

Even at *The Rodent's Gazette,* everymouse was excited.

So when Mousella came running to my

office, announcing that there was a new letter for me, everyone gathered to see what it said.

"Open it, open it! Open it!" they chanted.

"Okay, okay," I said, fumbling to open the ENVELOPE.

If you want to succeed in the second challenge, you will have to run three laps on the marked course. The race begins at eight a.m. tomorrow morning. Don't be late!

Another **PHYSICAL** challenge? I am not an **ATHLETIC** mouse. Why couldn't the challenge be eating as many grilled cheese sandwiches as you could in a sitting? Sigh. I let the letter slip from my 🐾🐾🐾🐾.

Creepella picked it up and **flipped** it over. "Look, Geronimo — there are more details here. You have to run all **THREE** laps in under eighty minutes!"

"B-b-b-but . . . that's such a **long** run to do in so little time!"

My sister, Thea, raised her paw. "I volunteer to transform my brother into an athlete! He'll be in good paws with me!"

Before I could utter a word, she dragged me to the MouseGym Fitness Center.

When I walked in, I heard whispering.

"Isn't that Geronimo Stilton, editor in chief of *The Rodent's Gazette*?"

"I heard that his next challenge is a race!"

"Really? He's already out of breath and he hasn't even started yet!"

My fur blushed Pink with embarrassment.

Thea waved her paw in the air. "Don't listen to them, Geronimo! Go put your workout clothes on and let's get started!"

When I returned, Thea clapped her paws together. "You look marvemouse! Are you ready?"

"Hmm . . . to be honest . . . not really!" I said.

But Thea didn't seem to hear me. "Let's start with fifty push-ups!"

I groaned. "Shouldn't we start small? What if I do some gentle stretching first?"

Thea shook her SNOUT. "We have less than twenty-four hours to whip your tail

into shape for the **CHALLENGE** tomorrow."
She put her **WHISTLE** in her mouth and . . .

PHWEEEEEEEE!

With that loud blast from her whistle, we were off!

I started my push-ups while my sister kept count:

"One, two, three . . ."

When I got to fifty, I was beyond exhausted. "I am so tired. I need to rest."

Come on, get going!

But Thea blew her whistle again. "We're just getting started! Now I want to see you jog one hundred laps around the gym."

This is so hard!

Holey Swiss cheese,

Thea was taking this training thing a little too seriously!

Halfway through, I collapsed on a mat, huffing and puffing. "Is . . . it . . . time . . . for . . . a . . . water . . . break . . . yet?" I said between gasps for air.

Thea **GLARED** at me. "Absolutely not. We can't let you be outsmarted by some admirer, can we?"

I looked thoughtful. "Maybe we can?"

"That would be bad for Creepella's business — and for *The Rodent's Gazette*."

My whiskers shook. "Fine!" I groaned. "Let's just finish, then."

Thea CHEERED. "That's the spirit!"

Crusty cheese niblets! I had to be successful tomorrow . . . if I survived Thea's workout!

READY, SET, GO!

The following morning, I walked to the starting line at the harbor. The streets were **crowded** with rodents eager to **WATCH** the race.

A rodent held up a sign with my name on it. She CHEERED me on. "We are all with you! You can do this, Geronimo!"

I **laughed**. "Thank you, I sure hope so! If I win, someone should throw a cheese party!" But the rodent looked serious.

Another mouselet next to her nodded. "That is a *fabumouse* idea. If anyone can pull a party together quickly, it's **CREEPELLA**!"

Before I could say anything else, a third rodent shook his **SNOUT**. "Don't get carried away. He's probably not going to make it to the end of the race, anyway."

"Hey!" I squeaked. But I could see Thea waving me over to take my place. I headed to the starting mark.

"You're going to do **GReat**!" Thea said. She slapped me on the back and I winced. I was still sore all over from our **workout** yesterday.

The loudspeaker roared: "**MR. STILTON, ARE YOU READY?**"

Creepella waved at me from the VIP seating. "Good luck!"

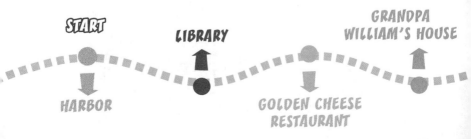

I got into position and waited.

"READY, SET, AND . . . Goooooooo!"

I started to run. The race kicked off at the harbor, continued past the library, passed by the Golden Cheese Restaurant, and then passed Grandpa William's house. He bellowed from the window as I huffed by:

"RUN, RUN RUN!!"

I ran and ran and ran.

I ran past the Mouseon Movie Theater, the mall, and the football field. I ran until I was back at the **HARBOR**.

The announcer rejoiced. "Unbelievable, dear listeners! Geronimo Stilton has completed the **FIRST LAP** around New Mouse City in just twenty-five minutes. If

MALL

PORT

OUSEON MOVIE THEATER

STADIUM

FINISH

he keeps this *PACE* up, he will SUCCEED! But . . . can he? I'm really not sure!"

Holey Swiss cheese, I wasn't sure I could do it, either! After one lap, all I wanted to do was collapse like a pile of shredded mozzarella.

Thankfully, as I ran by Thea, she handed me a parmigiano energy bar. "Here you go, Geronimo. Eat this; it's an energy snack."

I wanted to thank her, but all I could say was "Huff, huff!"

"Next lap I will give you another one!" Thea called after me.

Knowing that I had another **delicious** snack in my future gave me the strength to finish the second lap around New Mouse City.

I heard the loudspeaker CRACKLE to life.

"This is incredimouse! Geronimo Stilton has finished his **SECOND LAP**!"

I was so out of it, I could barely understand a crust of what he was saying! I just kept RUNNING and RUNNING and RUNNING, thinking of nothing!

To my surprise, I had just about finished my third lap! I couldn't believe it! The end was finally in sight. But suddenly, one of my paws landed on something soft, yellow, and squishy. A banana peel! My paw slipped

out from under me, and I **slammed** onto the ground just before the finish line.

The loudspeaker **CRACKLED** to life again. "Oh no! Geronimo Stilton has gone down like a wheel of hard cheese, just feet from the finish. The clock is still ticking. If he can't make it back up and across the line soon, he'll **fail** the challenge!"

A **hush** fell over the crowd.

I struggled to get back to standing — and then slipped on the peel again!

GREASY CAT GUTS!

A loud **buzzer** filled the air. "That's it," the announcer said. "He's out of time. He missed it by a whisker." The crowd groaned.

I struggled to stand again and tossed my headband to the ground in frustration.

Who had left the BANANA peel right in the

middle of the course? It hadn't been there in the first two laps—I was positive!

This was the second time someone had ruined my chances! What rascally rodent would want to see me fail?

I took a guess and squeaked out loud: "I bet **Hercule Poirat** had something to do with this! He loves BANANAS!"

But Hercule was out of town on a mission, so it couldn't have been him.

Something about all this still smelled stinkier than rancid ricotta.

But regardless of my suspicions, the verdict was the same:

SECOND CHALLENGE: FAILED!

HAVE A HEART, GERONIMO!

The big race was a FLOP! To make things **worse**, I still had to go to work at *The Rodent's Gazette* right after.

Grandpa William shook his snout when I came in. "Your performance today was a total **disaster**! I don't want the Valentine's Day *Rodent's Gazette* edition to be a total **disaster**, too!"

I didn't, either! I scurried back to my office. My desk was covered in piles of articles that needed to be read and edited. Then there was the special **Valentine's Day** insert that had to be rewritten. And I had to decide where the advertisements would go. Not to mention, I still had an editorial to write. Squeak, it was a cheddar mountain-sized amount of work!

"Yikes! I will be stuck here all **NIGHT**!"

Suddenly, I noticed an **ENVELOPE** smack in the middle of my desk. Could this be the **third challenge** already?

GREASY CAT GUTS! I was tired of these mysterimouse envelopes. With trembling paws, I opened it and read:

If you want to succeed at the third challenge, you must go on a treasure hunt.
You will walk up and down many streets to solve all the clues!

Go to the great obelisk in Singing Stone Square tomorrow morning at eight a.m.
Good luck! This is your last chance!

The next morning, I woke up **bright** and *early*. I was so tired, but I had to get going. Today was *Valentine's Day* — and the day of the big treasure hunt.

When I arrived to Singing Stone Square, I could see that Creepella's secret admirer had taken care of everything. A crowd had gathered. There were cameras and reporters.

A reporter approached me. "Tell us,

Yawn . . .

How are you feeling?

Geronimo, how do you feel this morning? Excited? Energetic? Nervous?"

I opened my mouth to reply, but only a YAWN came out.

Just then, Benjamin and Trappy ran over. "Uncle G, you look tired!"

"Thanks a lot," I replied. "I have been working two jobs, you know!"

Benjamin tugged on my elbow. "You better get started! The first clue is at the foot of the obelisk! And it's a RIDDLE!"

I followed Benjamin to the obelisk. I grabbed the letter waiting there and read it out loud. "Here you'll find good things to eat; sweet and juicy, what a treat!"

I wrinkled my snout. Lots of places in town had good things to eat.

"Maybe by 'good things to eat,' the riddle means good for you," Benjamin suggested.

My whiskers **perked** up. "Benjamin, I think you must be right! I think the next clue is going to be at the **fruit** market!"

Benjamin let out a **squeak**. "Let's go!"

Once I got to the **market**, I looked everywhere. I searched through apples,

pears, bananas, oranges, pineapples . . . until finally, under a huge pomegranate crate, I found the second clue.

It read: rodents come here to have fun; to find the next clue, you must run!

What could that possibly mean?

I tapped my paw on my snout. Suddenly, it came to me! "Of course! **The Amousement Park!**"

I took off to my next destination and quickened my pace. Oof, here I was running again! The park was all the way on the other side of town. By the time I reached my destination, my knees were trembling like **fresh ricotta**.

Once there, I started my search.

First, I hopped on the super-fast

sightseeing train with panoramic windows. No clue there. Then I checked each **roller-coaster** car. I had to ride it ten times and my head was spinning like a top! No note. Next, I tried the spinning teacups.

Ugh, I don't like going around and around like that. No note there, either!

Finally, I got up the courage to try the haunted house ride. And there was the next clue! Right inside a creepy coffin!

I was so scared, my fur turned as pale as a slice of provolone cheese. I read the clue out loud to myself: "a snack fit for a king; this taste really makes you sing!"

Hmm. I did not even have a tiny crumb of an idea for this one.

Clutching the clue, I left the amousement park and started walking back toward the center of town.

The sun was setting, and I was one run-down rodent. I hated to admit defeat, but it was starting to look like challenge number three was a BUST.

I slowed to a stop. Something smelled

delicious! What could that be?

I looked up to see that I was standing right outside the **MOUSEUM OF CHEESE!**

Cheddar-sprinkled sundae with bread crumbs on top! This was it! This had to be the place mentioned in the clue!

I raced over to the entrance. "One ticket, please!" I said to the young ratlet behind the register.

He **GRINNED** at me. "Of course! You are Mr. Stilton, editor in chief of *The Rodent's Gazette*, aren't you?"

"Yes, I am. Why?" I asked.

"I have been waiting for you!" he said, smiling. Then he handed me a **scroll** tied with a **RED** ribbon.

Squeak . . . what could this be???

I groaned. "Oh no, not another clue! I'm finished!" But with shaking whiskers, I unrolled the scroll and read it.

Holey Swiss cheese! I did it! I really did it! I hugged the Mouseum of Cheese ratlet and ran as **FAST** as my paws could take me back to the square.

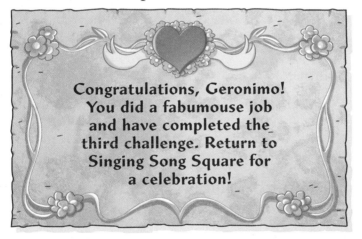

Congratulations, Geronimo!
You did a fabumouse job
and have completed the
third challenge. Return to
Singing Song Square for
a celebration!

A Celebration . . . and a Confession

When I went back to **SiNGiNG STONE SQUARE**, I was welcomed by a round of applause.

"Congratulations!" a rodent in the crowd yelled.

I melted like a cheese sandwich on a **HOT** grill. Literally! I had done so much running. Just as I held the scroll up over my snout in triumph, a wave of dizziness passed over me. I fainted **SPLAT** on the ground.

When I came to, **CREEPELLA** was hovering over me. "I am so glad you are okay. I watched the whole thing on the television monitor! You were so *fabumouse*. I knew you would not let me down! How would I be able to run the agency without you?!"

"Um, thank you," I mumbled.

Just then, the reporter **jammed** a microphone in my snout.

"Mr. Stilton, no one, absolutely no one, believed in you. However, against all odds, you did it! Now we want to know something: Do you know who this mysterimouse admirer is?"

I **peeled** myself up off the pavement. "I'm not sure, to be honest," I said, shrugging.

"I know!" a familiar voice **boomed** from across the street.

It was my cousin **Trap**. Every rodent in the square turned around to look at him.

The reporter ran to him, waving her microphone under his snout. "Come on, **tell us**. We have to know!"

Trap cleared his throat. He **wrung** his paws together. "It was me! I was the one who wrote the *letter*!" he cried.

My snout dropped open at the news. **"YOU?"** I said.

Trap looked apologetic. "I didn't mean for it to get so out of paw. I just wanted to play a **PRANK**!"

I shook my snout at Trap. "Some **PRANK**! I nearly wore my paws off running all over town."

"I was *jealous*," Trap admitted. "I wanted

to work with Creepella. But then she chose you as her Romance Consultant! Even after I'd done all that **work** for her launch party. And

It was me!

I thought you'd do a **bad** job and mess up her new business. But maybe you're not as much of a cheddarhead as I thought!"

"Trap! I can't believe you'd do that," Creepella said, looking disappointed. "If you wanted to be involved that **badly**, you should have asked. I would have found something for you to do."

"I was wrong — and you were great, Geronimo!" Trap said.

I stuck out my PAW and we shook on it. The crowd erupted in CHEERS again, and the sky lit up with fireworks.

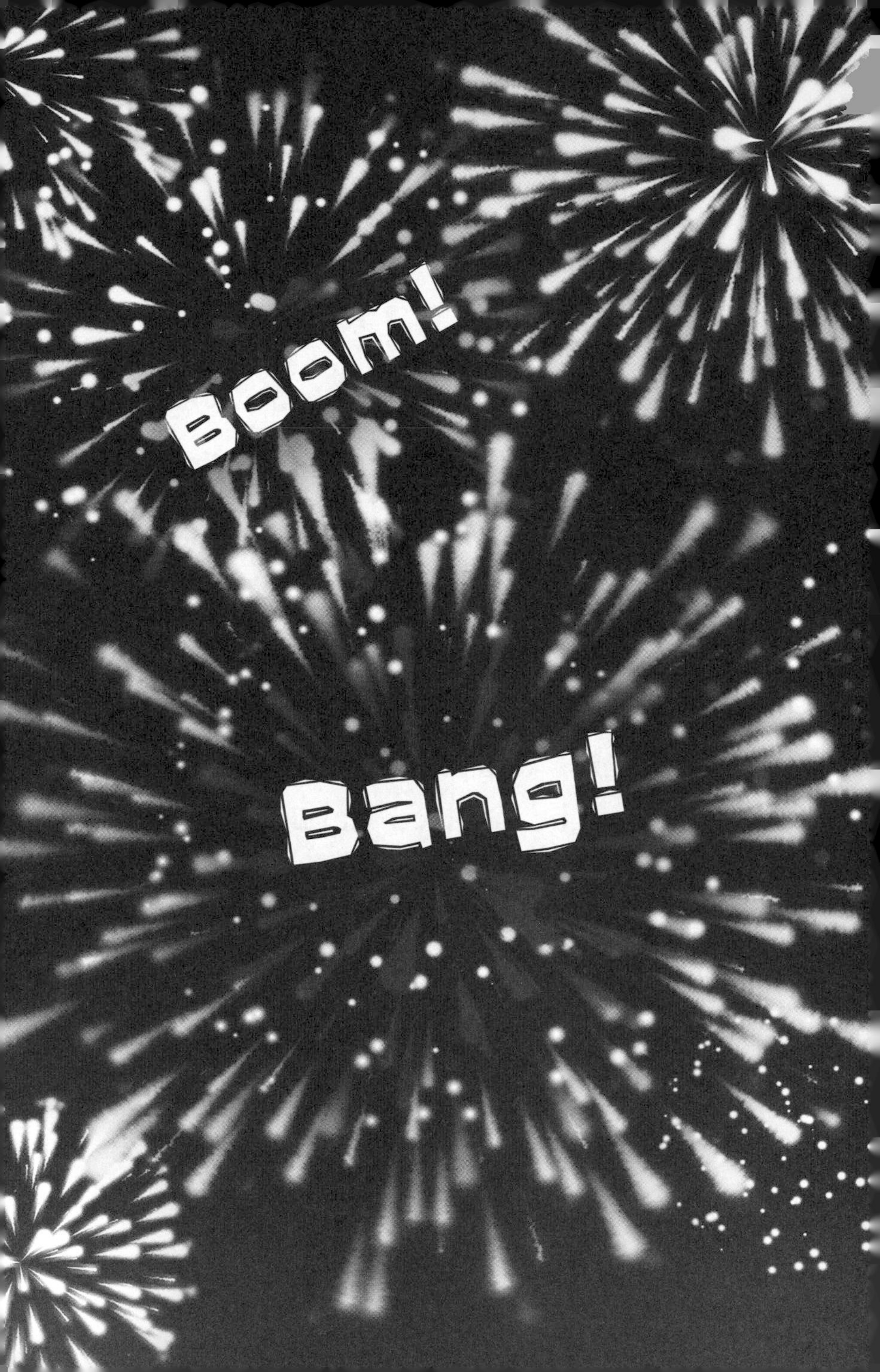
Boom!
Bang!

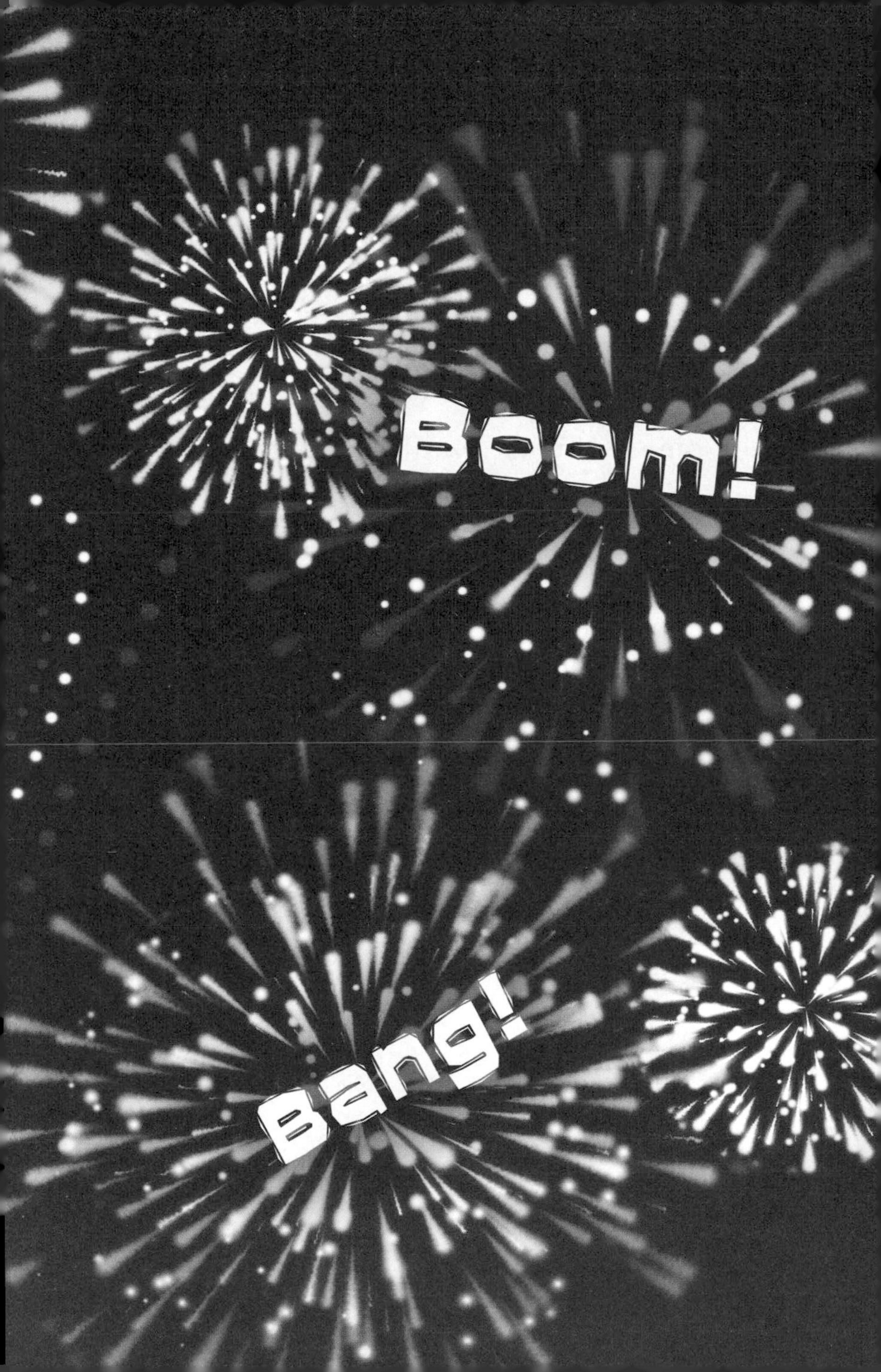
Boom!
Bang!

"Yippie for Geronimo! Yippie for Creepella! Yippie for Heart to Heart!"

It was a fabumouse fireworks show!

New Mouse City's citizens were so proud of me. Everyone wanted to **congratulate** me and sign up for the agency.

Creepella had been right. Trap's little prank might have been **annoying** for me, but it was clearly generating a lot of publicity for Creepella's business.

"I really want to find someone who loves to travel!"

Another one squeaked: "I would like a **wedding in outer space**. Do you think Creepella could make that happen?"

Squeak! If anyone could make these **dreams** a reality, it was Creepella!

A Rodent's Work Is Never Done

After all that excitement, I just wanted to go home and sleep for a long time. Once the **reporters** had packed up and the crowd had left, I yawned. "Well, that was mouserific, but I'm going to head home now."

Grandpa William shook his whiskers. "Not so fast, Geronimo! There is **work** to be done at the newspaper . . . *The Rodent's Gazette* doesn't take vacations!"

I sighed. "Okay, I'll swing by the **OFFICE** before I head home," I said.

Creepella grabbed my arm and handed me a stack of **new** applications.

"Since you're going to the office, would

you mind logging these new clients into the computer system? You're the best!"

With a **groan**, I headed back to the office. At least I could *enjoy* a little nighttime peace and quiet!

As I walked back through town, I could see rodents enjoying the evening. Some strolled paw in paw along the street. Others enjoyed romantic candlelit dinners inside restaurants.

Sigh!

Then I remembered, it was **Valentine's Day**! No wonder all the mouselets had **romance** on the snout.

When I finally reached my office, I sank down into my desk chair with a **happy** squeak. It was nice to **relax** after all that running around! But then my eye caught that mysterimouse **CASE X** folder lying out on my desk. Now was my chance. I had to see what was inside.

With trembling paws, I opened the folder. Inside was a **single** sheet of paper. On the paper was a **single** word:

Surprise!

As I read the word aloud, the room erupted around me with a chorus of voices, all shouting,

"SURPRISE!"

Everyone was there! Creepella, Trap, Benjamin, Trappy, Flora, Thea, and Grandpa William.

Creepella held my paw. "This is our **Valentine's Day** gift to you. A nice evening spent with everyone who loves you. Case X was a surprise for you all along!"

Creepella's thoughtfulness made my **heart** melt into a puddle of fondue. "This is so nice!" I squeaked, my eyes tearing up.

"Grandson, did you really think that we

would want you to come back and do work all alone on Valentine's Day?" Grandpa **boomed**.

"What a mouserific *Valentine's Day* idea," Thea said.

"It really is," I agreed. "But I'm afraid I don't have gifts for any of you!" I twisted my tail in my paws.

"Don't be a worryrat, Geronimo," Creepella said. "Your gift was the brave way

Yum!

Delicious!

you completed all those **CHALLENGES** for me and my business."

Just then Trap arrived. He brought with him a **huge** tray full of cheddar shakes.

"That looks *fabumouse*!" I cried.

Trap handed the first one to me. "It's the least I could do. Drink up, Cousin — you deserve it!"

I took the shake, squeaked, "Thank you!" and took a sip.

YUCK!!

It was disgusting. "What's in this thing??" I cried.

Trap giggled. "Limburger cheese! Just a little prank, cousin! You know me — I will never change, even on **Valentine's Day**!"

I groaned and tossed the shake.

"Don't worry, Geronimo! I brought you a real one, too," Trap said. "Your favorite — cheddar and chive!"

It's Limburger!!

Gross!

"Thanks, Trap," I said. I looked around my office at all the happy, smiling snouts. I was a pretty lucky rodent to have friends and family to celebrate **Valentine's Day** with.

Everyone likes to say that Valentine's Day is the biggest day of the year to celebrate romance. But really, it's about love and friendship, too. And it's important to **CELEBRATE** that every single day! From now on, every day will be **Valentine's Day** in my **heart**.

Love to all you dear readers from Geronimo Stilton!

Don't miss a single fabumouse adventure!

Up Next:

You've never seen
Geronimo Stilton like this before!

Get your paws on the all-new
Geronimo Stilton
graphic novels. You've gouda* have them!

*Gouda is
a type
of cheese.

Don't miss any of my adventures in the Kingdom of Fantasy!

THE KINGDOM OF FANTASY

THE QUEST FOR PARADISE:
THE RETURN TO THE KINGDOM OF FANTASY

THE AMAZING VOYAGE:
THE THIRD ADVENTURE IN THE KINGDOM OF FANTASY

THE DRAGON PROPHECY:
THE FOURTH ADVENTURE IN THE KINGDOM OF FANTASY

THE VOLCANO OF FIRE:
THE FIFTH ADVENTURE IN THE KINGDOM OF FANTASY

THE SEARCH FOR TREASURE:
THE SIXTH ADVENTURE IN THE KINGDOM OF FANTASY

THE ENCHANTED CHARMS:
THE SEVENTH ADVENTURE IN THE KINGDOM OF FANTASY

THE PHOENIX OF DESTINY:
AN EPIC KINGDOM OF FANTASY ADVENTURE

THE HOUR OF MAGIC:
THE EIGHTH ADVENTURE IN THE KINGDOM OF FANTASY

THE WIZARD'S WAND:
THE NINTH ADVENTURE IN THE KINGDOM OF FANTASY

THE SHIP OF SECRETS:
THE TENTH ADVENTURE IN THE KINGDOM OF FANTASY

THE DRAGON OF FORTUNE:
AN EPIC KINGDOM OF FANTASY ADVENTURE

THE GUARDIAN OF THE REALM:
THE ELEVENTH ADVENTURE IN THE KINGDOM OF FANTASY

THE ISLAND OF DRAGONS:
THE TWELFTH ADVENTURE IN THE KINGDOM OF FANTASY

THE BATTLE FOR THE CRYSTAL CASTLE:
THE THIRTEENTH ADVENTURE IN THE KINGDOM OF FANTASY

THE KEEPERS OF THE EMPIRE:
THE FOURTEENTH ADVENTURE IN THE KINGDOM OF FANTASY

Don't miss any of these exciting Thea Sisters adventures!

Thea Stilton and the
Dragon's Code

Thea Stilton and the
Mountain of Fire

Thea Stilton and the
Ghost of the Shipwreck

Thea Stilton and the
Secret City

Thea Stilton and the
Mystery in Paris

Thea Stilton and the
Cherry Blossom Adventure

Thea Stilton and the
Star Castaways

Thea Stilton: Big Trouble
in the Big Apple

Thea Stilton and the
Ice Treasure

Thea Stilton and the
Secret of the Old Castle

Thea Stilton and the
Blue Scarab Hunt

Thea Stilton and the
Prince's Emerald

Thea Stilton and the
Mystery on the Orient Express

Thea Stilton and the
Dancing Shadows

Thea Stilton and the
Legend of the Fire Flowers

Thea Stilton and the
Spanish Dance Mission

**Thea Stilton and the
Journey to the Lion's Den**

**Thea Stilton and the
Great Tulip Heist**

**Thea Stilton and the
Chocolate Sabotage**

**Thea Stilton and the
Missing Myth**

**Thea Stilton and the
Lost Letters**

**Thea Stilton and the
Tropical Treasure**

**Thea Stilton and the
Hollywood Hoax**

**Thea Stilton and the
Madagascar Madness**

**Thea Stilton and the
Frozen Fiasco**

**Thea Stilton and the
Venice Masquerade**

**Thea Stilton and the
Niagara Splash**

**Thea Stilton and the
Riddle of the Ruins**

**Thea Stilton and the
Phantom of the Orchestra**

**Thea Stilton and the
Black Forest Burglary**

**Thea Stilton and the
Race for the Gold**

**Thea Stilton and the
Rainforest Rescue**

**Thea Stilton and the
American Dream**

**Thea Stilton and the
Roman Holiday**

**Thea Stilton and the
Fiesta in Mexico**

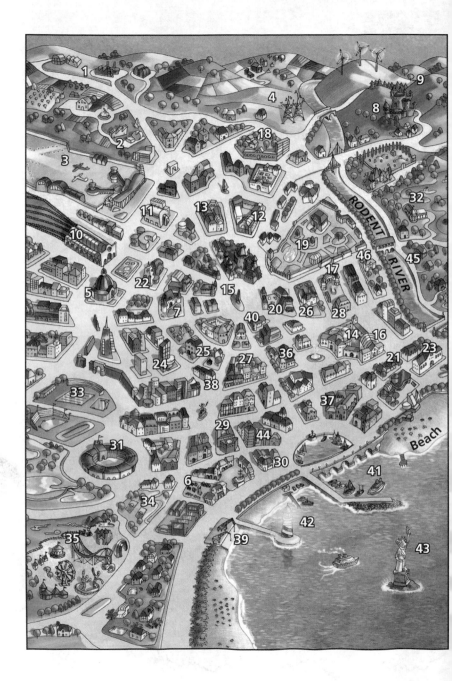

Map of New Mouse City

1. Industrial Zone
2. Cheese Factories
3. Angorat International Airport
4. WRAT Radio and Television Station
5. Cheese Market
6. Fish Market
7. Town Hall
8. Snotnose Castle
9. The Seven Hills of Mouse Island
10. Mouse Central Station
11. Trade Center
12. Movie Theater
13. Gym
14. Catnegie Hall
15. Singing Stone Plaza
16. The Gouda Theater
17. Grand Hotel
18. Mouse General Hospital
19. Botanical Gardens
20. Cheap Junk for Less (Trap's store)
21. Aunt Sweetfur and Benjamin's House
22. Museum of Modern Art
23. University and Library
24. *The Daily Rat*
25. *The Rodent's Gazette*
26. Trap's House
27. Fashion District
28. The Mouse House Restaurant
29. Environmental Protection Center
30. Harbor Office
31. Mousidon Square Garden
32. Golf Course
33. Swimming Pool
34. Tennis Courts
35. Curlyfur Island Amusement Park
36. Geronimo's House
37. Historic District
38. Public Library
39. Shipyard
40. Thea's House
41. New Mouse Harbor
42. Luna Lighthouse
43. The Statue of Liberty
44. Hercule Poirat's Office
45. Petunia Pretty Paws's House
46. Grandfather William's House

Brigand's Isle

This way to the Rodent Straits

Tomcat Island

Pirate Ship of Cats

Hamster Islands

Blue Dolphin Bay

Cat's Claw Bay

Panther Archipelago

Coral Reefs

Swissville

This way to the Mousific Ocean

Stray Cat Harbor

San Mouscisco

Cheddarton

Mouseport

This way to the Ratlantic Ocean

New Mouse City

Mousefort Beach

N
W · E
S

Furflung Island

This way to the Sea of Mice

MOUSE ISLAND

Map of Mouse Island

1. Big Ice Lake
2. Frozen Fur Peak
3. Slipperyslopes Glacier
4. Coldcreeps Peak
5. Ratzikistan
6. Transratania
7. Mount Vamp
8. Roastedrat Volcano
9. Brimstone Lake
10. Poopedcat Pass
11. Stinko Peak
12. Dark Forest
13. Vain Vampires Valley
14. Goose Bumps Gorge
15. The Shadow Line Pass
16. Penny Pincher Castle
17. Nature Reserve Park
18. Las Ratayas Marinas
19. Fossil Forest
20. Lake Lake

21. Lake Lakelake
22. Lake Lakelakelake
23. Cheddar Crag
24. Cannycat Castle
25. Valley of the Giant Sequoia
26. Cheddar Springs
27. Sulfurous Swamp
28. Old Reliable Geyser
29. Vole Vale
30. Ravingrat Ravine
31. Gnat Marshes
32. Munster Highlands
33. Mousehara Desert
34. Oasis of the Sweaty Camel
35. Cabbagehead Hill
36. Rattytrap Jungle
37. Rio Mosquito

Dear mouse friends,
Thanks for reading, and farewell
till the next book.
It'll be another whisker-licking-good
adventure, and that's a promise!

Geronimo Stilton